T0210091

THE JOLLY WOODMAN

THE TRUE STORY OF THE FIRST CHRISTMAS TREE MARKET IN AMERICA

WRITTEN BY JOANNA KELLY

ILLUSTRATED BY KATIE ATKINSON

AuthorHouse™
1663 Liberty Drive
Bloomington, IN 47403
www.authorhouse.com
Phone: 1 (800) 839-8640

© 2019 Joanna Kelly. All rights reserved.

No part of this book may be reproduced, stored in a retrieval system, or transmitted by any means without the written permission of the author.

Published by AuthorHouse 08/15/2019

ISBN: 978-1-7283-1751-9 (sc)

Print information available on the last page.

This book is printed on acid-free paper.

Because of the dynamic nature of the Internet, any web addresses or links contained in this book may have changed since publication and may no longer be valid. The views expressed in this work are solely those of the author and do not necessarily reflect the views of the publisher, and the publisher hereby disclaims any responsibility for them.

authorHOUSE®

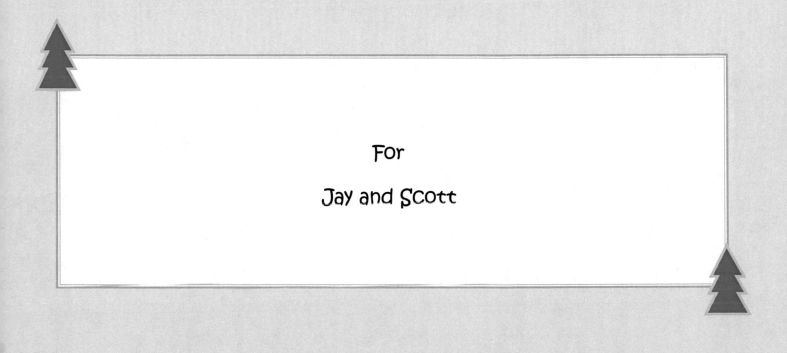

For

Jay and Scott

Dear Christmas tree in your holiday dress,
In your wildest dreams did you ever guess,
In your forest home so far away,
That you would be standing here today.

Jesse Cannon Eldridge

In the weeks before Christmas many years ago, a woodman named Mark Carr and his two sons trudged through the snowy forest looking for the perfect Christmas tree. The tradition of placing a tree in a church or a house had just caught on, and countrymen all over eastern America were bringing home trees and lighting them with tiny wax candles.

It was so cold that Mark and his sons could only stay outside long enough to see a few of the trees growing around their modest farm in the Catskill Mountains. Although densely populated with tall oaks and other hardwood trees, there was an abundance of pines, spruces, and balsam firs. The thick and spicy evergreens were well-formed and just right for the Carr's holiday parlor.

"Papa," said Mark Carr's eldest son, "come see this one. It's the biggest, and it has the best shape."

"Look at the one I found," cried the second son. "It's bushy and has strong branches to hold all those cookies mama made. Let's cut this one, Papa."

Mark Carr pulled his green scarf from his lower face, revealing a wide, warm smile. "You know," he said thoughtfully, "we are fortunate to have all these trees to choose from. Consider city children who must go without because they have no place to chop down a Christmas tree."

Their long faces showed Mark that his sons were truly sorry that boys and girls who lived in big cities couldn't have Christmas trees.

"Maybe we could bring them some of ours," the boys said almost together. Their eyes lit up as they looked hopefully at their father.

"New York City is nearly 80 miles from the Catskill Mountains where we live," said Mark. "How could I alone cut down all those trees and transport them through ice and snow to the river boat for the trip down the Hudson River?"

"You're right, Papa. It was a silly idea," the younger son said sadly.

"It looks like more snow is coming. We'd best get back home. We'll search for our tree again tomorrow," said Mark with a merry look in his eye.

"I'll look for an even bigger tree than the one I found today," said the younger son eagerly.

"Me too," returned his brother in a loud voice.

A small amount of snow fell that night, but it was enough to leave powdery puffs on the widespread branches of all the firs.

The woods were very quiet when Mark and the boys resumed their search for their Christmas tree. Deer tracks dotted the snow near their yellow farmhouse. Father and sons left their footprints in the snow, just as the deer had done during the night. With every step, Mark marveled at the glittering firs and thought about what an abundant harvest could be had.

Trees such as these would surely gladden the hearts of city children. Mark thought to himself. There's no such thing as a forest floor in the city, just cobblestone streets shaded by cold, high buildings.

By lunchtime Mark and the boys had chopped down a pleasantly-plump spruce that was so heavy it took all three of them to drag it through the woods and onto the porch. It was the third year the family had put up a Christmas tree, and this tree was the finest they had found.

The brothers stomped the snow from their feet and stepped into the cozy parlor to warm themselves by the fire. Mark stayed outdoors for a few minutes to look up at the cascade of evergreens that blanketed the mountain behind his house. Impressed by the wealth of trees growing on his land, he was suddenly motivated by the money he could make selling them. There had been a bad crop that year, and there was no work in the lumber mills that stood next to frozen streams. He had no job and was very short of cash.

"Yes," Mark said, looking up at the firs, "selling these trees might be a good way to make a winter living. Besides, all children should have a Christmas tree." In that moment he knew what he had to do.

That night, after the boys were fast asleep, Mark talked to his wife about his idea. She did not take to it kindly.

"What a foolish notion," she said sharply. "Don't talk such nonsense."

"New York City needs cut trees now that it's become fashionable for people to bring them into their homes and decorate them. We have a large supply around our farm, and I could make money selling them."

"Who would buy trees when they are free for the taking?" she asked in a piercing tone. "I don't want to hear another word about it."

In all the years they had been together, Mark had never heard such harsh words from his wife. Still, the idea nagged at him. When he realized there would be little money left for food or Christmas presents, he made up his mind to sell the trees without his wife's blessing.

"We'll help you, Papa," said the boys the next day.

"I can go to the barn and get the oxen ready for the trip," exclaimed the older boy.

"I'll help you with the oxen," offered his brother. "Then we can bring out the sleds and go with papa to chop and load the trees."

"Thank you, my sons," said Mark, patting each one gently on the head. "You will both be useful. Together, we will get the job done."

Mark made a plan and carried it out carefully. He marked all the trees to be cut and, early one morning two weeks before Christmas, he sharpened the tooth blades of his bow saw and cleaned his axe until it sparkled. The next day, with his sons' help, he cut down 36 trees and piled them neatly on the sleds. Some were tall; others were small; and the remaining trees were full and fat, like Santa himself.

"If one axeman can fell as many as 70 logs a day, we can certainly manage three dozen trees," said Mark to his boys as they tied the firs securely to the sleds.

Mark placed a wooden beam, called a yoke, between the pair of oxen to enable them to pull the heavy load. Now they were ready for the long journey to New York City.

Mrs. Carr watched as he yoked the oxen and connected the sleds, but she said not a word when they started off with their fragrant crop.

Slowly, slowly, the oxen pulled the evergreens over rough roads and deep snow to the banks of the Hudson River. When they got to the steamboat landing, they saw a boat that transported large numbers of people and goods all the way to the city.

From early colonial days, many towns in the area of the lower Catskill Mountains had some kind of trade on the Hudson River, but Mark Carr was the very first to trade Christmas trees.

"We'd sure like to go with you, Papa," said the boys to their father. They had never been away from home or visited a city. How exciting it would be to go all the way to New York City on a Hudson River steamboat.

Mark did not have enough money to pay for his sons' passage. Instead, he sent them back through the woods to the farm where they would be safe and warm until his return.

"I'd just as soon you go on home to your mama," Mark said as he pulled their woolen caps over their ears. "It makes a man proud to have children like you. I could not have done this without you, and I am very grateful. Now, take the oxen, and go safely."

Mark had been so busy cutting trees he didn't realize how nervous he was. What if this venture fails? he thought. Afraid that no one would buy his trees, he sat by himself and worried about what might happen when he arrived in New York.

The journey took several hours. When at last the boat arrived at the pier in New York, Mark had the trees sent over to the Washington Market. It was a huge center, which sold food and produce from all over the world.

Mark soon noticed that life in the city was bursting with activity. It was very different from his quiet country home in the mountains. As he wandered into the Washington Market, he saw several dozen vendors selling fruits and vegetables and row upon row of stalls with colorful and enticing food. Fresh-killed turkeys hung from hooks overhead and could be purchased for 12-cents a pound. Hams, sausages, and sides of beef, adorned with pink and yellow roses, awaited city shoppers. Mark was hungry and decided to try a fried cornmeal and sausage mixture called Philadelphia scrapple.

Mark saw many kinds of wreaths and garlands for decorating, but there was not one Christmas tree for sale anywhere. He walked up one block and down another looking for the right place to sell his trees. Finally, he found what he hoped would be the perfect spot. A shiny silver dollar bought him a strip of sidewalk on the corner of Greenwich and Vesey streets.

He untied his trees, and stood the pines and spruces next to the balsam firs. Soon customers flocked to his corner to examine his woodland wares.

"Fresh-cut Christmas trees," he roared as curious New Yorkers dug into their pockets for money to buy a tree. "Christmas trees for sale! Bring home a tree, and surprise your children on Christmas morning."

Mark's inventory quickly dwindled down. "Christmas trees for sale," he repeated. Soon there were only six trees left. Suddenly there were three. And then he was all sold out. He had earned a tidy sum and had enough money to get through the winter and to buy presents for his family.

To celebrate his success, Mark spent some time touring New York before returning home to the Catskill Mountains in time for Christmas.

When he arrived at the steamboat landing, his sons were waiting. "Papa, Papa, tell us about the city. Did you sell all the trees?"

"Yes, indeed I did," he answered with a twinkle in his eye. "I found buyers willing to pay high prices. And it was your hard work that made it possible."

"What's in the bags, Papa?"

"Oh, just a turkey and some fruits and spices for your mama. And I think there might be a few surprises for the best sons a man ever had."

The boys hugged their father and looked at him with anticipation. "Can we help you carry the bundles, Papa?" asked the older boy.

"Thank you," replied Mark as they approached their house. "You can take the smaller bags. No peeking! There will be no peeking before Christmas."

"We promise," they said excitedly.

"I've brought back a chestnut-fed gobbler for Christmas dinner," Mark said to his wife with a resounding laugh. He stepped inside the warm house and proudly held up a large, plucked turkey.

"There are few holiday things I love more purely than the Christmas turkey," said Mrs. Carr as she welcomed her husband home with a smile. "Except perhaps those beautiful trees in our own forest."

The family had the best Christmas any of them could remember. There were lots of presents under the cookie-covered spruce tree. Mark's favorite was a fine red sweater Mrs. Carr had made to say she was sorry for not believing in him.

The next year, Mark went back to the Washington Market with even more trees, and again he sold each and every one. From this small beginning, his tree business grew and grew. For the next 50 years, Mark Carr or his two sons could be found selling trees on the same corner the week before Christmas.

There were many changes since Mark had paid an old-fashioned silver dollar for his sidewalk space in 1851. By 1900, one in five American families had a decorated tree. The Christmas tree market had grown to over 200 thousand trees from the Catskill region alone. Thousands more came from competitors from as far away as Maine and Canada.

There were so many trees that they were stacked like cordwood, reaching as high as second-story windows. So great was the supply, they blocked out the sunlight, forcing shopkeepers to turn on their lights in the middle of the day.

Today, the Washington Market is gone; steamboats no longer travel up and down the Hudson River; and there is no one to remember that, once upon a time, a man named Mark Carr believed that children everywhere should have a Christmas tree.

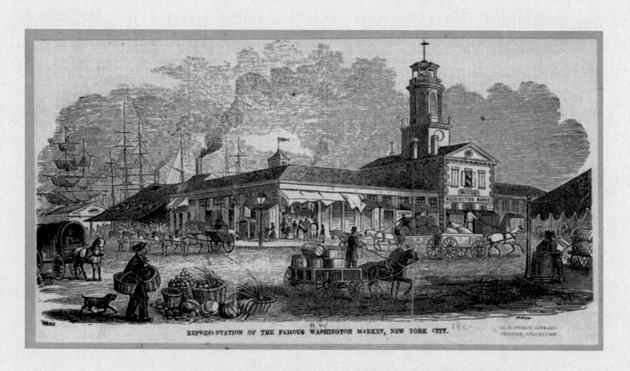

REPRESENTATION OF THE FAMOUS WASHINGTON MARKET, NEW YORK CITY.

The Washington Market, New York City.
Library of Congress, Washington, DC.

About Mark Carr and the Washington Market

The Washington Market got its start in 1812 and operated until the 1960s. It stretched over 12 blocks and became the largest market in North America. It gave way to redevelopment and to the site that became the World Trade Center.

On December 23, 1822, the Reverend Clement Clarke Moore went by sleigh to the Washington Market to purchase a Christmas turkey for his family. It is told that on the way he composed his beloved poem, "A Visit from Saint Nicholas," also known as "'Twas the Night Before Christmas."

Mark Carr became such a familiar figure at the Washington Market, the *New York Times* referred to him as *The Jolly Woodman*. They also reported that his sons were still selling trees on the same corner some fifty years after their father's first trip to New York.

By 1900, *House Beautiful*, one of the leading magazines of the time, said that "Mark Carr's little Christmas tree stand now rents for several hundred times what he paid for it."

Although the green markets of Lower Manhattan were selling holiday garlands, no one thought to sell a real Christmas tree until a Catskill Mountain farmer named Mark Carr took a chance and started a holiday tradition.

Load of Christmas Trees, New York City.
Library of Congress, Washington, DC.

Christmas Tree Facts from the National Christmas Tree Association

- Every year, there are approximately 25 to 30 million real Christmas trees sold in the US.
- There are close to 350 million real Christmas trees currently growing on Christmas tree farms in the US. All have been planted by farmers.
- North American real Christmas trees are grown in all 50 states and Canada. According to the US Commerce Department, 80 percent of artificial trees worldwide are manufactured in China.
- Real trees are a renewable, recyclable resource. Artificial trees contain non-biodegradable plastics and possible metal toxins, such as lead.
- There are more than 4 thousand local Christmas tree recycling programs throughout the US.
- For every real Christmas tree harvested, one to three seedlings are planted the following spring.
- There are about 350 thousand acres in production for growing Christmas trees in the US; much of it is preserving green space.
- There are close to 15 thousand farms growing Christmas trees in the US, and over 100 thousand people are employed full-or part-time in the industry.
- It can take as many as 15 years to grow a tree of typical height (six to seven feet) or as little as four years, but the average growing time is seven years.
- The top Christmas tree producing states are Oregon, North Carolina, Michigan, Pennsylvania, Wisconsin, and Washington .

Joanna Kelly was a staff reporter and historical feature writer at Citizen News, Fairfield County, Connecticut before serving as assistant director at Kent Memorial Library in Kent, Connecticut. She is the author of Hooligan's Alley, The Man Who Loved Kennedy, Tomato Pie, Written in Stone, and The Wildflowers of Sherman, Connecticut. Joanna lives in Litchfield County, Connecticut.

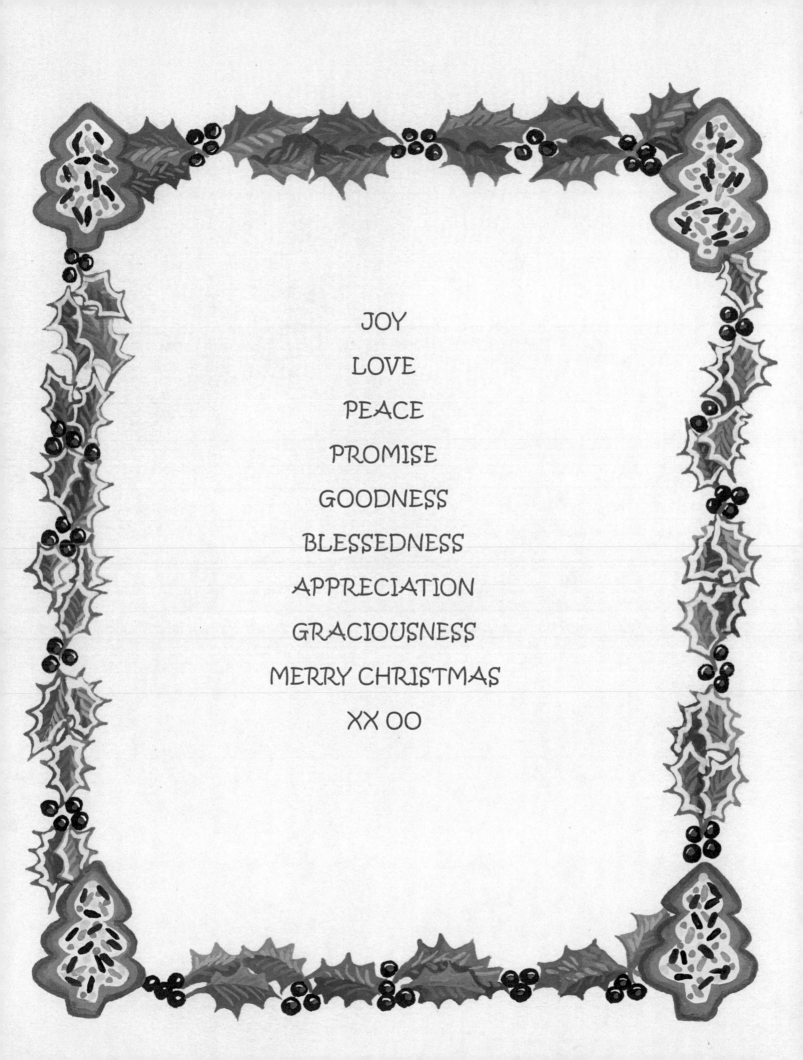

JOY

LOVE

PEACE

PROMISE

GOODNESS

BLESSEDNESS

APPRECIATION

GRACIOUSNESS

MERRY CHRISTMAS

XX OO

Printed in the United States
By Bookmasters